Old Mr. Mackle Hackle

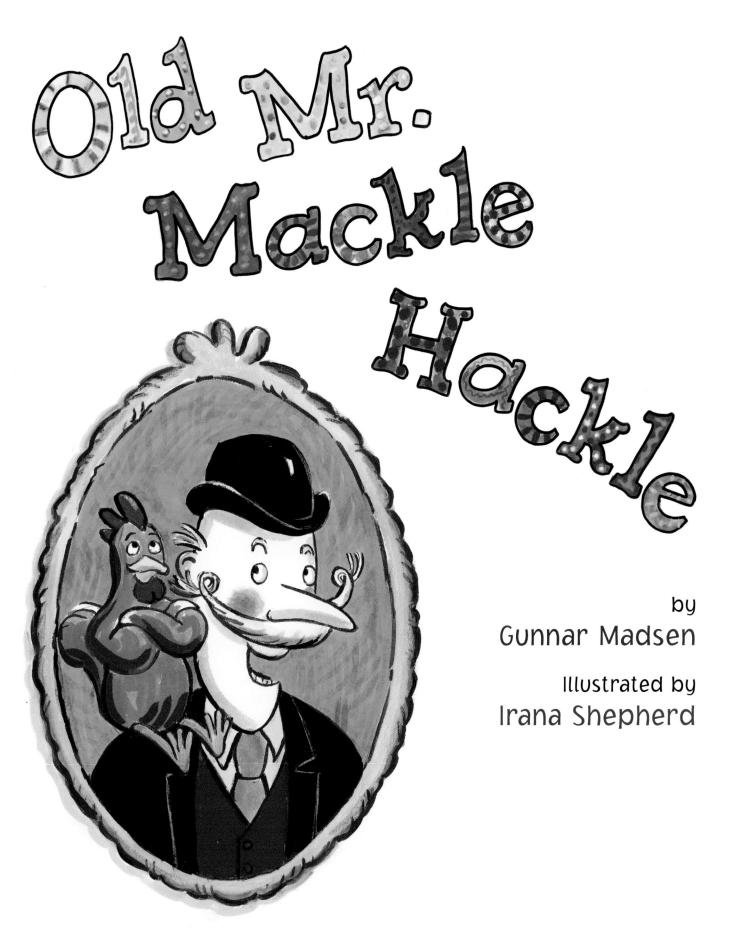

by
Gunnar Madsen

Illustrated by
Irana Shepherd

LITTLE, BROWN AND COMPANY
New York ❧ Boston

Little, Brown and Company

Time Warner Book Group
1271 Avenue of the Americas, New York, NY, 10020
Visit our Web site at www.lb-kids.com

First Edition

Library of Congress Cataloging-in-Publication Data

Madsen, Gunnar.
  Old Mr. Mackle Hackle / by Gunnar Madsen; illustrated by Irana Shepherd. — 1st ed.
    p. cm.
  "This story is based on the song 'Old Mr. Mackle Hackle' by Gunnar Madsen, Richard
Greene, and Ruth Kirschner. . . . The song is from a collection of songs for children written
by Ralph Pack" —T.p. verso.
  Summary: Old Mr. Mackle Hackle is concerned when his hen will not cackle, so he takes
her to a doctor and a fortune-teller, and even tries telling her chicken jokes, but once her
chicks are hatched the tables are turned.
  ISBN 0-316-73452-7
  [1. Chickens — Fiction. 2. Farm life — Fiction. 3. Animal communication — Fiction. 4.
Humorous stories. 5. Stories in rhyme.] I. Shepherd, Irana, ill. II. Title.

PZ8.3.M26701 2004
[E] — dc22

                                                                    2003054633

10 9 8 7 6 5 4 3 2 1

Book design by Saho Fujii

PHX

Printed in China

The illustrations for this book were done in fluid acrylics on Strathmore Aquarius watercolor paper.
The text was set in Jacoby-Light, and the display type was hand-lettered.

For Quinn, my mighty love
—G.M.

For Morgan, who, when he was eight, wrote:
You haven't lived intill you've chased chickens
—I.S.

Old Mr. Mackle Hackle

had a hen that wouldn't cackle

He took the hen to Dr. Boyce
The doctor said, "She's lost her voice!"
The doctor said a brand-new beak
would fix her up so she could squeak

"She cannot squeak, she's got to cackle!"

said Old Mr. Mackle Hackle

He took the hen to Madame Mack,
a fortune-teller draped in black

She reached inside her magic sack
and found a piece of old hardtack
The chicken gobbled up the snack,
turned her back, and gave a . . .

"Hens shouldn't quack. They've got to cackle!"

said Old Mr. Mackle Hackle

He ran downtown and found a book
called *Chicken Talk* by Doctor Snook
He cracked it open—**"Holy smokes!**
This book is full of chicken jokes!"

He got goose bumps and chicken skin
and broke out in a crazy grin

"Come, my little chickadee,
I'll make you cackle, tee hee hee!"

"If you feed your chicken cement, what do you get?

A bricklayer!"

"If your chicken lays an egg on top of the barn, what do you get?
An egg roll!"

"How does a chicken bake a cake?
From scratch!"

"What do you call a crazy chicken?
A cuckoo cluck!"

"What happened to the chicken whose feathers pointed the wrong way? **She was tickled pink!**"

"Why did the chicken cross the basketball court? **She heard the referee calling fowls!**"

"What did the doctor say to the sick chicken? **You've got the people pox!**"

The hen flew up into the air
Her feathers fluttered everywhere
She gave a squeak! A squawk! A quack!
She shouted, "YAKKITY YAKKITY YAK!
GIVE ME PEACE, SOME QUIET TIME,
I'M SICK OF ALL YOUR JOKES AND RHYMES!"

"Now hold on here!" said Mackle Hackle

Just then, they heard a tiny crack
Old Mackle Hackle's jaw went slack

"Crackle?" said Mr. Mackle Hackle
"Crackle!?"

crickle,

crackle,

peck,

and scratch

A dozen eggs began to hatch

A large one cracked and opened wide
A chick popped out—"Hi, MOM!" he cried

moaned old Mr. Mackle Hackle

The mother and her chickadee
together whispered secretly
The chick perked up, his eyes went wide
"THAT'S WHY THIS GUY IS SO TONGUE~TIED?"

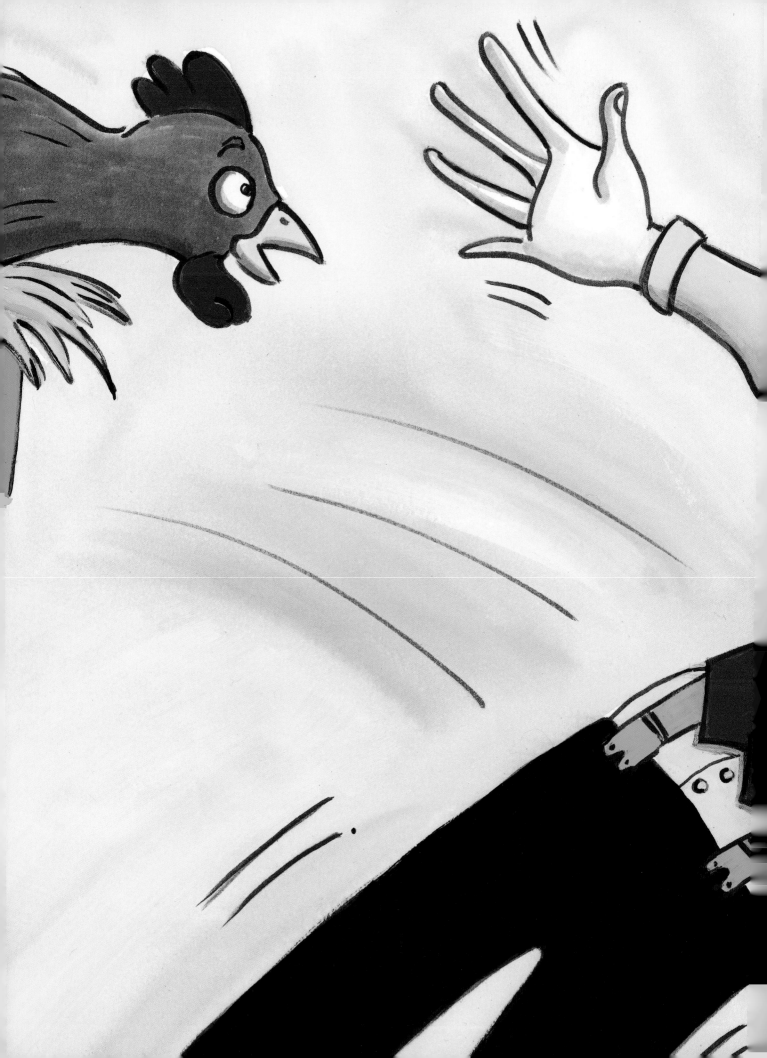

And with a cricking, cracking sound

the eggs hatched open all around